Mark Edwards

PIRATES ON DINOSAUR ISLAND

Mark Edwards, playwright and author of short stories, teaches writing and media studies at Sacred Heart University in Fairfield, Connecticut. His play "Ladies in Hats" was a Kennedy Center semi-finalist and appeared in The Boston Theatre Marathon. His story "Last Call" was published in *The Last Man Anthology*, and "The Man Who Shot Bigfoot" can be found in *Space and Time Magazine*.

First published by GemmaMedia in 2012.

GemmaMedia
230 Commercial Street
Boston, MA 02109 USA

www.gemmamedia.com

© 2012 by Mark Edwards

Printed in the United States of America

16   15   14   13   12   1   2   3   4   5

978-1-936846-09-2

    Library of Congress Cataloging-in-Publication Data
Edwards, Mark, 1966–
    Pirates on Dinosaur Island Mark Edwards.
        p. cm. — (Gemma Open Door)
    ISBN 978-1-936846-09-2
    I. Title.
    PS3605.D8897P57   2012
    813'.6—dc23

                                        2011049172

Cover by Night & Day Design

Inspired by the Irish series of books designed for adult literacy, Gemma Open Door Foundation provides fresh stories, new ideas, and essential resources for young people and adults as they embrace the power of reading and the written word.

Brian Bouldrey
North American Series Editor

GEMMA
Open Door

I know not what to call this, nor will I urge that it is a secret overruling decree, that hurries us on to be the instruments of our own destruction, even though it be before us, and that we rush upon it with our eyes open.

—Daniel Defoe,
Robinson Crusoe (1719)

1

The Author finds himself at the mercy of dire and bloody circumstance.

I awoke to the slaughterhouse smell of blood and the sulfur stink of gunpowder. There were muffled cries and a cold internal voice told me, "Your hearing is nearly gone from standing too close to a twelve-pound cannon, and those are cries of the wounded, and when you open your eyes you will wish you hadn't."

I did open my eyes. The deck of the brig was carnage. Fiercely armed men rushed about, blood flowed from the scuppers, spars were shattered and splintered, a mast and sail had crashed onto the foredeck, and a score of wounded and dead were scattered about.

I could not see out of my left eye, and I reached up expecting the worst to find that I merely needed to wipe a clot of blood from the lid. There was a painful cut above my ear, most likely caused by a flying splinter. My last memory before fainting was of a ball smashing the frame of a nearby gunport.

Any relief I felt at finding my skull intact immediately vanished as a large fellow in a patchwork coat loomed over me, aiming a pistol between my eyes. He wore a grin that would have been rakish if he hadn't cocked the pistol.

"Hold ye," said a voice from behind me. "They say this one's the surgeon."

A tall man limped into view, long of leg and pigtails, gripping a cutlass. There was grey in his beard and blood on his

2

black coat. He pushed aside the other's weapon and leaned over me, speaking in a loud fashion, as if he kenned my fuddled state. "You can live, if ye'll stitch and dose our wounded."

I don't know where my courage came from, since I thought I'd left my honor back in England. "I'll physic your men if I can physic my own," was my response.

"You can." The tall man glanced about the deck. "What's left of 'em."

That is how, reluctantly, I came into the service of Captain Baltizar.

2

A duel with an unexpected outcome, flight, and a voyage.

I came to be on a floating slaughterhouse amidst the Caribbees due to a lack of five hundred pounds a year and a misplaced pistol shot.

I had faced William Brucknell on the Downs; two gentlemen of honor, two pistols, two seconds, two rivals, two fools. The Brucknells owned the Downs and most of the land nearby, and William was the first son and heir of Lord Brucknell; magistrate, horse breeder, and drunkard. I was the son of nobody, but had been to University and learned natural history, the mathematics of medicine, and the arts of surgery. William had five hundred pounds a year, and would inherit more soon, considering the gross state of his father's liver. I had a practice worth forty a year, a small cottage, a bay horse, and my own wits.

William was less bright than his horses, and also nearsighted, which was why, in that moment of malice when he challenged me, I had chosen pistols.

It was over a woman. Penny had chosen to affiance wealth over wits, and I had said so in front of witnesses. And so misty dawn on the Downs, dew on our boots, pistols loaded, and each of us awaiting the order to fire. Grass before breakfast.

I had not slept the night before, knowing what the outcome must be. I was a fair marksman—well practiced in collecting animals for study—and by dawn I decided that I did not wish to kill William. As we turned towards each other, pistols raised, I decided to shoot him in the right shoulder after he had

5

missed, to cause minimal harm and yet satisfy honor.

William panicked and immediately upon the command to fire, shot off my right earlobe. I pulled the trigger in shock.

I saw the blood gout from above the bridge of his nose. He was dead before his second reached him, and I was on my bay riding towards Portsmouth before they had his corpse home. It does not do to kill the son of a magistrate and peer.

It would be a poor physician who took long to find a craft willing to take him on. Ships often have surgeons who began their careers as barbers, apothecaries, or butchers. In Portsmouth I had offers of positions and berths within two hours of my arrival. I chose the privateer *Worcester*—a trim eighteen-gun brig—not because of the obvious ship-shapeness of the vessel and the cheerful authority of the captain, but because they sailed on the next dawn to the Spanish Main. Our business would be to harass and take the shipping of Spain and battle buccaneers and other enemies of His Majesty King Charles wherever they could be found.

I spent the rest of that cool, bright spring day at the port selling my horse, completing my medical kit and sea chest, dodging doxies, and writing three letters to Penny, each in turn torn up, all in a mood of general remorse. I set sail with such remorse the next morning, despite the fine wind, the wine-dark sea, and the prospect of new experiences.

3

*Of ships and surgeries and an
accidental amputation.*

Captain Jonathan Hakes was insane, by any standard other than that of the fighting men who sailed. He would attack a ship of double the *Worcester*'s guns, since he had long before decided that the fighting qualities of an Englishman were worth thrice that of a Spaniard or freebooter. By the time we had reached our cruising ground on the Main, we had already taken four ships, and there had been much work for my needle, scalpel, and bone saw. Hakes was a brave man of considerable generosity and wit who believed himself invincible, as did many of our crew. He was good company to your narrator.

When we met Baltizar's *Smoke 'n'*

Oakum, a ship of thirty-eight guns and a crew of five-score buccaneers, somewhere in the latitudes south of Cuba, the arithmetic of odds offset the triple courage of our English tars. Captain Hakes was also unaware that the *Smoke 'n' Oakum* was rotting from keel to the gunwales, and the crew was fighting desperate to take a ship that wasn't sinking.

I performed surgery for sixteen hours after the *Worcester* was taken. I became so exhausted that I required the surviving ship's boy to mark wounded limbs with an X so I would not amputate the wrong ones. The *Worcester* had gone into battle with a crew of fifty-two, twenty-eight of whom were now dead, including Hakes and his first mate. Twelve more were severely wounded.

Of the pirates, fifty-three were dead or overboard, and another score had need of my skills—a high price for their new brig. Another eighteen men from both parties would die that night, some on the table before me, some in the mortal hour before dawn.

While I did my work across a bloody slab made from three sea chests, the buccaneers transferred stores from their failing craft to the *Worcester* and repaired the damage to the ship, spars, and sails, putting our own hale crew members to work. The dead, including Captain Hakes, were wrapped in sailcloth and dropped overboard with cannonballs tied to their shrouds. The screams of my patients were punctuated by the shuffle of goods and men on deck, and the occasional splash of the dead dropping into the sea.

When I came on deck at dawn, I saw a transformed vessel, as near to trim as it had been before battle, except that our sailors were now replaced by buccaneers dressed in a mix of rags and finery. Here the long coat of a sea officer over ragged drawers, no shirt, and a brace of pistols; there a fellow in an embroidered gold jacket with a filthy kerchief on his toothless head. I knew enough by then to see that they were a seaworthy bunch of villains.

The man in the motley coat approached me where I stood by the starboard rail, and nodded in a kindly way. As I remarked at first sight of him, he was of cheerful visage and was a well-knit fellow of about thirty, with long moustaches and a crooked smile.

"All sew'd and bandag'd, yours and ours?" said he.

"Yes, I've done what can be done."

He drew his pistol, "Then *you're* done."

There is something to be said for exhaustion: it creates a sanguine acceptance, a carelessness. I struck the pistol from his hand before I knew what I was about, and was bearing him to the deck before *he* knew what I was about. He was the stronger, and despite my advantage from being on top, he was strangling me.

I still had a lancet thrust into my belt. I drew this and slashed at him, more to frighten than to harm, and he frantically threw me off. He rose, half-drawing a dirk, and I fearfully swung the small blade at him again. He staggered back, blood flowing down the hand he'd clapped to his face, and we both stared stupidly at his nose, which lay on the deck.

I became aware of the crowd around us, including the Captain, who picked up the fallen pistol and aimed it at my belly. He pulled the trigger.

4

A few observations on the nature of rough humor and the compromises we make to survive.

Having spent my share of time among some of the worst of humankind, I must insist that there is no greater evil in the world than a humorist who engages in practical jokes. Noseless Bill, formerly known as Patchwork Bill, was one of these creatures, who thought it witty to slice through the cord of sleeping seaman's hammock or piss in someone's grog or fire an empty pistol at a victim who believed it was loaded.

When Captain Baltizar pulled that trigger and I discovered that the gun had powder but no shot, I felt foolish for a moment, and then I felt rage. If Patchwork Bill thought there was humor in threatening a man, then the loss of a nose was the least he deserved.

The crew seemed to think so as well. Patchwork Bill had been popular among the rougher crew, who admired his pranks to avoid being victims of them, but all on deck found his maiming a cause for hilarity. Surrounded by laughing pirates, my spirit finally gave out and I sank to the deck. The last I heard before fainting were Bill's cries that I sew his nose back on.

I awoke in a hammock in what had been Capt. Hakes's cabin, and my first sight was of Baltizar devouring a ham and ship's biscuits at table. I must have made a noise, for he looked up, poured a cup of grog to which he added water, and brought it to me. He held the cup until I drank it down in short gulps. He then helped me to a bench at the tableside.

"You need to drink more, and eat, even if it's just a biscuit or two." He slid one towards me. "I've already tapped the weevils out of that one, can't be more than one or two in it."

I poured myself more rum. "How long was I unconscious?"

"Most of yesterday and last night. It's coming on dawn now."

The captain was somewhere between forty and fifty and of dark complexion. His beard was braided, he was broad shouldered, and his voice had the rough deepness of a smoker of tobacco. He had a chronic limp in his right leg which did little to impede his dexterity. I never discovered his real name, nor the origin of "Baltizar." Some said it was because he was of Moorish descent. Some said he was once as rich as a Biblical king. I found the first explanation to be pure guesswork. I detected a Scotch burr to the captain's accent, when in his cups, that suggested the highlands more than

Arabia. He was, I would learn, an expert navigator (a rarity among buccaneers), a lethal hand with a sword, and in most ways less bloodthirsty than Captain Hakes.

"I owe ye some thanks, Dr. Lemuel. There's a dozen of my men who would be at the bottom without you," Baltizar said.

"I do what I can to ease suffering, and saved your men so I could save my own." I attempted to sound haughty, but the cup in my hand shook.

"A good turn is a good turn, despite the cause," he said. "I've asked your crewmen about you. You killed a man in England, and are probably an outlaw. No family, no prospects, as you're a bastard —but you have talent."

The only person to whom I had told my story had been Captain Hakes, but it was impossible to have a private conversation on a brig thirty yards long.

"You seem an ideal candidate to join my crew," he continued. "Nine of your men already have. There's little difference in being a surgeon for a privateer and being a surgeon among buccaneers. Except for more silver."

I protested, and he parried each argument. In the end we agreed that I would continue my duties as surgeon until we reached a neutral port, to earn my keep and the safety of the remaining crew who hadn't joined. But I knew that we would have this argument again.

The captain allowed me to keep my hammock in his cabin for the remainder of our time together. At first I thought it was because he wished to convince me by proximity to join him. But it didn't take me long to realize that he was protecting me from Noseless Bill.

5

Of the nature and business of piracy.

Pirates are a lawless lot, at least where the rules of civilization are concerned. Any ship is fair prey, crews that resist are cheerfully massacred, and cargo and sometimes ships are taken. The Brethren of the Coast have their own code, with some variation from captain to captain and ship to ship. These were the laws that Captain Baltizar and his men subscribed to:

I. Every man has a vote in affairs of moment, except during engagement with the enemy; has equal title to the fresh provisions, or strong liquors, and may use them at pleasure, unless a scarcity makes it necessary, for the good of all, to vote a retrenchment.

II. No person is to game at cards or dice for money aboard ship.

III. To keep their muskets, pistols, and cutlass clean and fit for service.

IV. No boy or woman is to be allowed amongst them. If any man were to be found seducing any of the latter sex, and carried her to sea, disguised, he was to suffer death.

V. To desert the ship or their quarters in battle was to be punished with death or marooning.

VI. No striking one another on board, but quarrels may be ended on shore, at sword and pistol. The disputants to stand back to back, at so many paces distance; at the word of command, they turn and fire immediately. If both miss, they come to their cutlasses, and then he is declared the victor who draws the first blood.

VII. If any man should lose a limb, or become a cripple in their service, he was to have two hundred pounds, out of the public stock.

VIII. The captain and quartermaster are to receive two shares of a prize;

the master, boatswain, and gun-
ner, one share and a half; and
other officers one and a quarter.

These rules are what kept Noseless
Bill from my throat. As the captain's
guest I at least was to be treated as a
crew member, and he could not do violence to me while at sea. Some of the
men had warned me, should we find a
port, to stay on board.

Of their sailing ability, the quartermaster, a grey-eyed mulatto called Prester
John, the ship's master, and a dozen or
so of the crew were fine hands. Many
of the others could knot and splice and
haul a rope, but that was all. This rare-
ly mattered, for the crew could sail well
enough to deal with the seas and storms.
As for the maneuvering of battle, their

tactics were simply to quickly close in on a ship, to use cannons to shatter their foes, and board with dozens of screaming cutthroats.

I was to see these tactics used twice on this voyage, once against a French privateer of equal size and crew, and again against a Spanish merchantman that refused to heave to at the sight of our black flag. Baltizar let the French vessel think the *Worcester* was prey, and after being pursued for an hour used a change of wind to turn about and board after two exchanges of cannon fire. The merchantman, a larger ship but with few guns, surrendered a moment after the boarding.

After each battle Baltizar offered any able man a chance to join his crew, and often made up for men lost with men recruited. The French ship, which the captain thought too damaged to take, was left to its surviving crew to make their way home in as best they could. The merchantman's officers were set adrift in their ship's boats within sight of Surinam, and the ship was towed into Port Royal to be sold.

There were three other captures made, without resistance, while I was on board. Many ships on the Main knew that surrender was the lesser of two evils. To fight pirates could mean a battle without quarter. To let the pirates board without violence meant that you might keep your lives.

I did my duty as physician and surgeon to pirate and victim alike, and found more than one man among the crew who was grateful for my services. This would serve me in good stead later in my adventure.

6

A galleon that is not a galleon, a sea chase, and a storm.

Every pirate dreams of capturing a Spanish treasure galleon, full of gold from the mines of the New World. Captain Baltizar sailed us farther and farther south, chasing the rumor of a treasure ship, with a cargo rich in emeralds and amber and silver.

Eighteen days of fair sailing brought us in distant sight of a large ship at last. The crew readied for battle and the captain set a course to pursue. Prester

John watched it through a spyglass and declared that it was indeed a Spanish vessel.

It was a Spanish frigate, a ship of war with thirty-six twenty-four-pound guns, a crew of three hundred, and a commission to seek out and destroy all pirates.

The frigate came about suddenly, and in minutes was on our windward side and began its chase. In sea battles the ship that has the weather gage, which controls the windward side, can control the maneuvers. In half an hour a ship that had been two miles away was within five hundred yards, firing finely aimed cannon shots our way.

Baltizar took the ship westward, fleeing with the occasional splash of a cannon ball in our wake. In calm seas the small ship has the advantage of speed. In a wild sea the mass of a larger ship allows it to be faster. Its weight, combined with a greater spread of sail, allow it to cut easily through the waves. The sea was rough, the frigate gained on us moment by moment, and the fire of its bow gun became more accurate.

The *Worcester* had lost several yards, and I was already tending to wounded hands below deck, when the squall struck. Clouds had formed during the chase, and finally the clouds burst, with high winds and wild sea.

The frigate lost sight of us immediately, and the captain set his course for southwest, with three men at the wheel to hold the ship on course. I now had to tend to those breaks and falls that happened while men fought with sails and rigging during the storm.

In the night our mainsail yard snapped, two men fell overboard, and we lost our pursuer in the stormy dark. The wind calmed before dawn, and Baltizar, after a sleepless night on the quarterdeck, ordered most of the sails taken in. He no longer knew how far he was from the coast of the Main, and was sure that he could smell land.

Dawn found us with tattered sails, broken yards, and an exhausted crew, approaching a green island that lay beyond rocky shoals.

7

An island and an unexpected encounter with an unlikely creature.

Had I stayed on board, there would be a different tale to tell, but the captain was going ashore, and Noseless Bill remained aboard to help affect repairs. I thought it wiser to accompany the captain. The ship found anchorage in forty fathoms of water off the shoals, and only the ship's boat could enter the island's rocky bay. The shore party was to find a tree that had the makings of a new topsail yard, as well as to find provisions. The *Worcester* was low on water and grub.

So eight of us rowed into the harbor to find a sandy shore before us and jungle beyond. Our party included myself and the captain, Prester John, a young bosun's mate called Oliver, a hypochondriac named Jack who often sought my services, an oft-smiling pirate called Jolly, the grey-haired carpenter known as Chips, and a stunted, swarthy cut-throat known as Daft Barry. This last man was worrisome—he was a companion of Noseless Bill. I wondered if I imagined his constant malicious glare as we rowed in and landed on the beach.

There was a musket and plenty of shot and powder for each of us, in case we found game. There were also Chip's tools and a tent, as well as grog and other supplies. We unloaded and the men began to make a camp on a level space near the shore.

I found the naturalist in me awakening, and began examining the forest edge along the shoreline. In moments I found an orchid and two beetles I could not identify. Lost in my observations, I wandered a few hundred feet away from the rest of the crew. There I first saw one of the beasts.

A small stream exited the forest across the gravelly shore, and at its bank an enormous creature lowered its head and drank. It was a lizard of sorts, though I immediately noted that its legs did not splay outward. It was wide-bodied, with two rows of small spikes along the length of its back, and its short neck gradually shrank to a head which snorted and snuffed in the stream. The eyes were black with gold irises, its skin a mottled green on grey. It was ten yards long from tip of tail to nose.

After a moment it raised its head, blinked at me, and stomped off into the jungle. It left three-toed tracks in the sand. They spanned four times the length of my hand.

8

A discussion of what is and what is not, in fact, a crocodile.

"A crocodile," Chips said, prodding the fire.

"This was much more massive," I said.

"I paid a tuppence to see one in Surinam," Prester John said. "It was longer than a skiff." He draped strips of bacon over a green branch above the fire, where they dripped and caused the coals to flare.

"They say that on the African coast

the beasts can be larger than the one John saw." Baltizar looked up from his chart. He was trying to identify the island. "Tis' likely that's what you saw."

"But I have seen the skeletons of crocodiles and this was shaped nothing like one," I said. "The skull was much too small in relation to the body. And a crocodile will flee into water, whilst this beast went towards the jungle."

Daft Barry snorted. "Or the doctor has been tasting his own laudanum. Opium has made men see strange beasties afore this."

There was a general laugh at this, and I gave up trying to convince them. Instead I leaned close to the firelight to sketch and describe the beast in my notebook.

And then the roar filled the night, a great bestial howl, deep and rumbling. It came from the forest behind us, and was answered by another cry, further up the coast.

"I heard an alligator bellow in the Floridas," Baltizar said.

"Was it such a cry as this?" I asked.

He shook his head and turned his attention to dinner.

The ancients, when mapping far-off places and the strange lands visited by the adventurous, would mark the blank places on their charts with "Here there be Dragons." This, of course, has been taken for fear of the unknown and unmapped. It is now my belief that the ancients knew whereof they spoke.

9

*Of a dagger in the forest
and a grisly feast.*

The morning after the sighting of my creature, I set out with a musket to find some fresh meat. I also wished to track the beast.

It was simple to find a trail near the shore, but I was soon sidetracked by a large marsh. After bogging down and muddying myself to the knees several times, I skirted the marsh by moving through the edge of the jungle. Small beasts disappeared into the brush, but too quickly to identify. There were some birds in the upper branches of the trees and I paused from time to time to describe them in my notebook, which I then tucked into my belt beneath my shirt.

I had just finished such an observation when I heard a hail from behind me in the forest. Daft Barry was approaching. I immediately regretted leaving my musket just out of reach against a tree, but as his was slung across his shoulder, I relaxed.

"Sawbones—the captain sent me to watch out for ye," he said. I nodded, and then realized that Baltizar would be unlikely to choose one of Noseless Bill's friends to watch over me. As I stepped towards my musket, Daft Barry snatched a dagger from his belt, and with an overhand snap, threw it into my belly.

I felt no pain and had snatched up

my musket when he kicked my legs from under me. He crouched above, grabbing my hair with one hand and drawing out the dagger with the other. "Bill asked that I take your nose back to him. He didn't say I had to kill you afore or after."

At such moments the senses seem to sharpen, and I could see Daft Barry above me, every pore of his face, the sty in his right eye, his crooked incisors. The birdsong around us hushed. As he placed the edge of the dagger against my nose, I also saw the great shape rise behind him, the horns above the feral eyes and the fearsome jaws.

Daft Barry sensed too late the thing behind him, and half-turned when great jaws closed from head to ribcage and lifted him off me.

I had scratches on my arms and legs to prove that I had climbed the tree, rather than made some sort of miraculous leap. I perched forty feet above the earth and was fearful it was not high enough.

Daft Barry's screams were muffled inside the creature's maw. The beast shook the cutthroat and shattered his spine. It then dropped the bloodied corpse and howled the cry that we had heard the night before.

I had received several shocks in a few scant moments, and it took me a second or so to realize that I must be fearfully wounded. As a grisly feast went on below me I checked my belly, expecting a horrific dagger wound. Instead I found my journal, leather cover and pages pierced through by the force of the blade, and a minor scratch from the tip that had pierced skin but not gut.

Relieved, I turned my attention to the beast. Do not condemn me for making careful observations. Much of the horror was alleviated by the knowledge that Daft Barry had tried to murder me.

The creature was longer than the one I had spied the night before, and stood on two legs instead of four. I can compare its stance to that of a large bird, though different in that each movement suggested enormous power. Its head was fearsome: great blunt nose, wide jaws, finger-long teeth. A horn of eight or nine inches curved back from each eye. The skin was striped green on yellow in the patterns of the forest. It had three toes to a foot, and three fingers on its forelegs, which were so small that they were of little use as it fed. He ate without chewing, tearing off great bits of Daft Barry to swallow whole.

While this monster fed, a gathering of smaller creatures appeared from the forest, seven in number. They were much more birdlike, dodging about on two legs trying to join the feeding, and they had feathers behind their heads and along the backs of their forearms, as if they aspired to flight someday. The great beast snapped at them when they came into range, but they dodged nimbly, and one finally managed to carry off one of Daft Barry's hands while the others chased it into the forest.

I estimated that an hour passed

before the giant strode off towards the meadowlands. I waited another hour before climbing down. It was then that I heard the sound of gunfire from the coast. I snatched up my musket and ran towards the stuttering sound.

10

Of monsters and mutiny.

I had forgotten about the smaller creatures. I was reminded when one leapt from behind a tree directly into my path, jaws agape and clawed fore-arms raised.

I lowered the musket and fired, close enough to singe the beast with the muzzle flash. It fell aside with a squeal and another appeared at my side, and nipped at the back of my trousers. I half spun, swinging the musket like a club, and battered the creature end over end. Though five feet in length, it could not have weighed more than three or four stone. I turned in a slow circle, and watched the other five appear around me, heads lowered, circling, trying to keep at least one of their fellows behind me.

I slung the musket and drew the cutlass that I'd brought along to cut through brush. I heard two more shots from the direction of the coast, quieter than the pounding of my heart against my breastbone. I held the cutlass across my body, edge out. It would only be a matter of time before one leapt.

It was two at once. One jumped directly at my face, and as I swung the cutlass, another leapt upon my back. I saw a swirl of blood before me as I reached back to grab the creature by the neck, its hind claws tearing my flesh above my belt, and I leant forward and threw the beast towards the others, hitting another that snapped at me. One lay on the ground, lower jaw hacked off by my blade, and the others closed on it, squabbling and eating. I ran again.

I broke shore north of the camp, and saw in the bay another longboat approaching. The *Worcester* still lay outside the rocky entrance, and smoke rose from a gunport followed by the deep cough of a cannon. A ball splashed short of the longboat, and as I ran along the beach to the camp, another shot fell even shorter. After that, the ship was silent.

The boat reached the camp before I did, and I found general uproar. Here is what had transpired while I was inland:

Baltizar and his companions had found suitable a tree near the shore. Chips and Prester John and Jack set about cutting down the tree and then shaping it into the mast. Daft Barry had gone off to hunt. Baltizar and Jolly began to cut a trail to drag the mast to shore.

Baltizar, hacking at brush with his cutlass, had turned to say something to Jolly and found him gone, with only a splash of blood and some enormous tracks left where he had been. Baltizar rushed to find the others.

While shaping the tree with an adze, Prester John had looked up to see, high among the branches above him, a large head looking down at him. He followed the shape of the thing down the length of a long, snakelike neck, to a huge body, four tree-trunk legs, and finally a great tail that was longer still than the neck. He swore to me that the animal was twenty yards long. The beast looked stupidly at him for a few moments, and then began eating leaves from the upper branches of trees, pausing occasionally to make a small hooting noise. There were other such noises from inside the forest.

When the captain found the men, the creature was gone, but they managed to determine in a few moments that there were huge and dangerous beasts on the island, and they struck out for the shore.

Chaos compounds chaos. On board

the ship, Noseless Bill had convinced a dozen of the more vicious and stupid crew members to mutiny. They had struck before dawn, arming themselves and attacking the rest of the crew.

They were nearly thwarted by Old Jacob, the toothless man who wore the gold jacket. Jacob was a berserk combatant, and after the first shots were fired he had armed himself with a boarding axe and set upon the mutineers like a fury. Others of the crew followed him and drove the mutineers below decks. They turned a cannon on the main hatch to keep the villains below, and Old Jacob was preparing to signal the captain to return, when a mutineer who had climbed the rigging shot Jacob in the chest.

When Old Jacob fell, his men lost

heart and set out for shore with their wounded hero in the longboat. The mutineers tried to sink them, but they were out of cannon range by the time they regained the deck.

I struggled mightily to perform a miracle of surgery before the sun set—to remove a bullet from Old Jacob's body. The shot, alas, had pierced his liver, and he died under my knife, telling me that, "I've survived worse than this."

I looked up at the surrounding men, four watching, the other seven facing the menaces of the forest with muskets ready, and shook my head. I turned to look out over the bay, and saw the *Worcester* sailing off on the evening tide, the last of the sun lighting its upper sails.

11

*Of our resources and plans
for our survival.*

In the light of a fire that night, the pirates held an election. Baltizar was no longer captain of the ship, and it fell to the men to elect a leader on shore. I attempted to abstain from the voting but was overruled by the men—if we were to rely on each other for survival, we must join in all tasks together.

Each man who wanted to lead had his say, mixing braggardly eloquence with profanity. A vulgar little Yorkshireman named Sameal told us he possessed "cocksure tacticals and single-bloody-mindedness." Chips nominated Prester

John because, "He's part blackamore, and they're handy at livin' in jungles, ain't they?" Prester John stated that the nearest he'd been to a jungle before sailing on the Main was picking pockets near a caged tiger in St. Paul's courtyard.

Baltizar, for his part, stated that he had more wits and had killed more men than the whole lot of us, and if that didn't make for a captain on land as well as sea, he didn't know what did.

We voted by dropping stones into Prester John's hat, with the initial of the candidate on each. It was no surprise that there were eight *B*s in the hat when we counted. I received one vote—one of the more illiterate fellows had drawn a skull and jagged line on his pebble, and it took us a few moments to gather that this meant "sawbones."

We were twelve in number. We had a longboat and a skiff, twenty yards of canvas, six muskets, four pistols, forty rounds of shot, two kegs of powder, nine cutlasses, two axes, three boarding axes, an adze, a saw, two pouches of tobacco, six pounds of dried peas, thirty-two ship's biscuits, sixty fathoms of two-inch rope, sixty yards of fishing handline, nine fishhooks, five pounds of salt pork, three pounds of bacon, one half-full cask of rum, and one unopened bottle of brandy. Each man had a knife. Of my surgical tools I had only my small lancet, a heavy knife, and two curved needles. Our kit was sufficient for an outing of a few days, but not while marooned permanently on an island full of hostile beasts that had already killed two of our crew.

Baltizar took command in the same manner he did at sea. I know the inventory above because we made it the next morning, and he had me log it on the back page of my journal. I claimed the rum and wine for medical purposes. My companions stopped cursing me when I asked if anyone wished me to set a broken bone or perform a necessary surgery on one of them while he was sober.

Baltizar fashioned some new rules. No man was to go anywhere without another man with him, and one of each pair must have a musket. Night was to be divided into three watches of four men each. And each day half the party must explore some part of the island we did not know, to seek supplies. The shore party would fish and improve the camp.

It is to his credit that in the next three weeks that we only lost two companions. Micca Silver, a notorious sot, stole the bottle of brandy and crept off into the woods to enjoy it. We found his hat and the half-drunk bottle on a log not far from camp. Most of Micca had been compressed into a giant footprint. He must have fallen into boozy sleep on the ground and an enormous animal had stepped on him in passing.

The other, a fearsome fighter known only as Cutlass, died when a wound taken during the mutiny festered. He had been slashed across the upper arm and had not let me sew and dress the wound after the battle, trusting instead to a pinch of gunpowder in the wound. The infection claimed him from shoulder to fingertips in ten days, and when we finally held him down against his protests, I saw that the black and stink had spread to the muscles of his chest. Even amputation could not have saved him. It was to Cutlass that we gave the last of the brandy to ease his passing.

Besides securing the camp and hunting and exploring, Baltizar had a further plan: he wished to use the two longboats and native wood to construct a small craft that could sail us all away. He spent every evening of the first two weeks planning and arguing with Chips over how to build it, and on the third week, Chips pegged out the shape of a thirty-foot craft in the sand. We all stood around and looked upon it, in hope and also in fearful thought, each wondering, when the boat was finished, who would still be alive to sail in her.

12

*Of some of the great reptiles
that we habitated with.*

I managed to convince Baltizar to allow me to accompany the explorations. I was most competent to find fruits that were edible, and most likely to have some insight into the island's creatures. It is from these explorations that I compound this bestiary.

The great predator that had killed Daft Barry, because of its horned head, was called "the hungry bull" by the pirates. On occasion we were stalked by one, but they seemed loath to approach four or five of us, despite their enormous size. I shudder to think of how easily the monsters could have disposed of us had they the courage. It would have taken volley after volley of musket-fire to kill one. These animals seemed to be solitary, and I saw no more than three individuals on our time on the island.

The gigantic long-necked creatures—which Prester John called "jennies," after a paramour from his past, strode about in several herds, eating the leaves of trees. The young, some as small as cattle, would travel at the center of the herds for safety. A pack of the small hunting beasts isolated a young jenny, and we witnessed an adult catching one of the hunters in its jaws and casting it a great distance.

These "hunters" were our chief trial. Singly and in small numbers they could be fought off, but an even dozen had attacked the immature jenny, and we were in dread that such a group would descend on one or two of us. They were bold enough to filch fish and game from our camp, and I awoke one dawn to find one trying to eat my journal. I brained it with a stone. The pirates took to wearing their feathers in their hats as a mark of the number they'd killed. The hunters had one advantage, which was that they were plentiful and of a size that made them fine for spitting and cooking over the fire.

Another carnivore gave us cause for

worry. It was half the size of the hungry bull, and much slimmer with a longish neck, small head and long jaws. It also walked only on its hind legs. These creatures were bold and stupid. One strode into camp, seized the seated boy Oliver by the boot, and tried to drag him into the forest. Prester John broke its neck with an axe. The pirates named them "lubbers" for their general foolishness.

The spiky beast I'd seen on our first night ashore we simply called a "hedgehog." They could be found on the forest edge, grazing on heavy grasses, and were almost entirely harmless, unless you approached them. Jack chanced upon a sleeping one in the forest that chased him into the bay.

There were huge, cow-like beasts that

lived in the meadows. We could never get close to them because the small herds fled when we approached. They had three horns and jaws like a turtle. I called them "trinocerouses." They had smaller kin, hornless, with jaws like parrots, which were no less shy and grazed in the meadowlands in great numbers. When I asked what they should be called, while we feasted on one we had fire-roasted, Oliver suggested "delicious."

There were two varieties of two-legged herbivores. One was the "duck-bill," much of the size and shape of the lubber, but an eater of marsh plants. The other was half that size again, an eater of fruit, from what I saw of it feeding and from the studies I made of its dung. These smaller creatures were perfectly mottled to match the forest leaves, and we were more than once startled to find ourselves standing amongst a dozen of them. These were the "invisibles."

There was also a crocodile, like the Surinam variety, but much larger. A sluggish river ran through the marsh and was populated by these monsters. This explained the reluctance of even the largest of the island's creatures to enter the water. We took care never to bathe where this river met the sea.

On the island it seemed as if every hairy creature that we knew of had been replaced with a reptile that served the same purpose as hunter or prey or grazer. The enormity of some of these reptiles, I can only guess, had something to do with the nature of the island itself.

13

*Of a great storm and the breaking
of our camp.*

Much of our time was spent with the work of survival: our camp grew, we built a small stockade fence on the shore side, the boat progressed in its slow building as Chips shaped lumber. We had meat enough to eat, and fruit enough to avoid scurvy. We used homemade bows and spears to hunt and preserve our scant ammunition; we fished with handlines and scoured the shore for shellfish. The large beasts spent more time in the interior, so the shore seemed safe enough.

The men, cutthroats and buccaneers, had settled into a tribal life with surprising calm. There were arguments, not surprising among men of blood, but even such dimwits as Squint could see that each needed to rely on the others' goodwill. Then came the storm.

Four of the men were fishing out in the harbor in the longboat one afternoon—the smaller skiff had already been sacrificed to build the new boat—when they began to pull towards shore. I ran to the shoreline, expecting to see some new creature pursuing them, when I saw on the horizon a thin line of dark grey. As the men rowed, the greyness became greenish and the darkness began to ascend into the sky. A sultry wind began to whip about, and I could see the distinct blue lines of lightning in the darkness.

Oliver stood beside me. "Can you feel it, Doctor? The air's thickening like a stew," he said.

"A storm?"

Oliver turned towards our camp, beyond the tideline, only a few feet above the sea level, unprotected on the seaside. "A bloody calamity," he replied.

The fishermen landed and ran ashore, led by Prester John. "We need to batten down!"

Baltizar came out of the tent, took one look at the sky, and began shouting orders.

Seamen know how to prepare for a storm. Loose tools and weapons were stowed in our few casks or the tent. Extra lines and pegs appeared and secured our belongings. I rushed about, packing my small medical supply an in oilcloth, wrapping up my journal and stowing it inside my jacket, and getting in the way of more competent men. By the time the sky had turned the color of strong tea and the first winds tore at the tent, all was battened down.

For four hours we huddled in the tent and the world outside went mad. The waves created something more than a roar, the wind screamed, and the forest behind us sounded as if it was being torn up by the roots. And then the real storm struck.

Had the hurricane not found us on the incoming tide, we might have weathered the night. But storm and tide combined and the first great wave soaked the sitting up to the chest and knocked the standing off their feet. The next wave was larger and we were suddenly afloat and at the mercy of a new sea.

It is unlikely but true: most sailors cannot swim. Among us only Jack, Prester John and I could do so. My last sight of the boy Oliver was his soaked locks disappearing into the black water and then I was swept inland. I slammed against someone or something in the dark, and finally I caught the trunk of a tree, which I held onto with desperate strength as wave after wave broke over me. The hot rain fell. I tried to climb higher, was nearly swept free, and so clung miserably in one place, trying to breathe between the crash of each wave.

I clung through the night, awake for terror of drowning if I dozed. It was late morning when the sea began to recede. Hunger, thirst and exhaustion were nothing to the stiffness and pain of my arms and legs. Water still pooled around my ankles as I unwrapped myself from the scaly bark of the palm, and immediately fell face-first into the brack. I rolled over and looked up at a towering lubber that was staring down at me.

I suspect that he was as waterlogged as I was, and storm dazed, or you would not be reading this. He lowered his head on that long neck and sniffed me repeatedly, then turned and staggered off, splashing, to the shore. I must have smelt less like meat and more like sea wrack.

I finally climbed to my feet, the sultry wind still blowing about me, and made

my own way towards the shore to seek
my companions.

14

Of the day after the storm,
and of becoming flotsam.

What was left of our camp, I found
not on the shore but in the forest: an
empty keg, a shattered musket, some
torn canvas, a dozen yards of cordage.
The tools of civilization were gone. I had
my knife, and a fairly sodden journal.
Of my companions there was no sign. I
picked up the musket and broke off the
remnants of the lock and stock and so
had a heavy steel truncheon.

On the shore I found some oysters
and other shellfish that had been washed

in by the storm. I left my journal to dry on the sand while I feasted on these raw. Full and exhausted, I foolishly lay back on the sand and slept.

It was past midday when I awoke, and it must have been instinct that brought me around. There was movement up and down the beach, and in the moment it took for the sleep to clear from my eyes, I was heartened to think it my returning companions. But hope turned to terror in less than a heartbeat—along the shore, picking up stranded shellfish as I had, were dozens of hunters.

They had not noticed me because of the quantity of other food. I was sure that they would change from picnickers to predators the moment I moved.

It is telling what possessions we

choose to save in moments of crisis. My truncheon was out of reach, and the wisest move would have been to rise, make a leaping grasp for it, and dash the five yards into the sea. Instead, while still lying prone, I reached with a forced slowness for my journal, wrapped it in oilcloth and, with exaggerated care, deposited it under a large rock. It was the clack of this stone against others that alerted the hunters to my presence.

That they nearly got me was because of a sleeping cramp in my calf as well as my foolishness. My imagined run for the waves became a stagger and then a fall into the surf, and as I struggled forward it was with a hunter's jaws attached to my ankle, doing its hungry best to hamstring me. I was able to get the other leg under me in the shifting sand and lunge further into the bay, but the hunter hung on despite being towed along.

At waist-deep the advantage was mine, and I strove to break the hunter's neck while it thrashed underwater and tore bloody channels into my arms with its claws. It finally released my calf and by then I had remembered my knife, so that when its head broke the surface I was able to stab it in the eye and then further into the brain.

On shore was a waiting mob of the creatures, standing in ranks and staring hungrily at me, a most unnerving sight. I pushed their dead companion towards them so that the next wave washed it to within their hungry reach. The shore erupted into a squabble for fresh meat.

I backed further into the bay and considered my situation. Before me was a platoon of hungry monsters. The sea was a haven from them, but I was bleeding from a dozen clawings and scrapes. There were sharks in the bay of the black-tipped variety, harmless enough when encountered singly, but soon to be drawn to my blood in toothy schools. If I swam north along the shore, I would reach the mouth of the river populated by crocodiles. If I swam south I would come against the rocky wall at that end of the bay, unclimbable at the best of times, and not something I could scale in my current state of exhaustion. But when three choices lead to being devoured alive, and the only other is an impossible task, the impossible becomes the only choice.

15

Of a climb and fever dreams.

If the climb took me a moment, it took me three hours. Had it not been for two occasions where I was able to rest for long minutes along crevices that allowed me to shift my weight from arms to legs and back again, I would have been food for the fishes and gulls. I left a quantity of skin and two fingernails on that cliff, and scraped off an eyebrow and broke the middle finger of my right hand in that hellish climb.

When I finally crawled over the edge

and onto the top of the cliff, prone and gasping, I wanted nothing more than to sleep there on the rocky surface. But I had been leaping from skillet to fire and back again since dawn, and so I forced myself to sit and look about for the next horror that I would have to face.

I was on a ridge that ran inward towards the center of the island to some rocky hills. I had been at the foot of these hills on our explorations; they were between the great marsh and some rocky uplands. Nearest to me, the ridge thinned out to a bridge that was broken into rocky prominences as it went inland. It was the safest location I had been all day. Some of the hunters had followed me for a short distance when I swam, but had then lost interest. And here I could see where our campsite had been, in case any of the others returned.

The distant hills looked to be another location worth exploring when I had more strength.

I had no hunger, but a great thirst, which I soon slaked in a pool of storm-water. I wrapped my broken finger as best I could in a strip of my shirt, and decided that none of my other wounds were dire enough to need attention. They had been cleaned by the salt water. It was still sultry, but there was a breeze, so I stripped off my clothing to dry and lay on the stone, which in my exhaustion was more comfortable than a mattress, and there fainted into a deep sleep.

It is only to be expected that soon it began to rain, accompanied by a biting wind, and so I spent the night shivering as the sea crashed below.

The next day dawned bright with sun, as did the next three. I was scarcely aware, as I was shaking and burning with fever, with just enough presence of mind to lie with my shirt over my head to lessen sunburn. In my fever delirium I saw again the blood burst from William Brucknell's skull. I saw as if I was there the horror on Penny's face when she heard the news, dreamed of gore-spattered decks and of endless hours of trying to reattach the limbs of shattered men. I dreamed that it was I who had died that day on the downs and all the subsequent madness was but my passage through hell where my fate would be to forever be hunted by scaly demons who pursue and devour me only for my tattered body to be reborn and hunted again.

On the third day I undertook, with shaking blade, to bleed myself to lessen the fever. I don't know if it was the bleeding, or the cooling of that night's air, but in the morning I awoke weakened but well. After a breakfast of gull's eggs I began to stagger along the rocky ridge towards the center of the island, feeling a hundred years old and two hundred years dead.

16

Of being observer and observed.

There were numerous reptiles amongst the rocks, tiny, unfeathered cousins to the hunters. They seemed to be hunting insects and stealing gull's eggs. They were too swift to capture, and when I rested, a few of them would approach and chatter to each other about me. The consensus seemed to be that I was too large to tackle.

I also discovered that the lubbers were primarily fishermen. I watched a dozen of them hunting along the banks of a stream, their heads dipping like herons, coming up with large fish. I should have known from examining their skulls—the long jaws and the narrow teeth.

As I traveled inland, the ridge widened and I climbed higher, wary now. A hungry bull, jaws half-open, turned its head to follow me as I passed on a ledge above it. There was no malice in its black eyes, just simple calculation. It would waste no energy leaping for something it could not reach. Still weak, I shivered and barely trusted myself to walk steadily until I had passed from the beast's sight.

At midday I was in sight of a rocky plateau, possibly a mile off, and I promised myself that I would reach it by nightfall. I could walk for five minutes at a time at this point without resting. The sun was setting behind the plateau as I made the last fifty yards uphill, and there I smelled woodsmoke. I staggered around a rock outcrop and I saw the fire and the three men seated around it. It was Jack who rushed forward to catch me as I collapsed, and I lay there looking up at him and Baltizar and Prester John.

Prester John pressed a gourd full of

water to my lips. Baltizar said, "Well here's the doctor, harder to kill than a dose of the pox."

Jack lowered me to a sitting position, "Belike, the captain means that as a compliment."

17

*Of courage and cravenness
and an escape.*

When the storm struck, Jack had been carried by the wave into the forest. He'd floated and swam until he had found a boulder near the stream we had used for water, and sheltered there, soaked but safe. Baltizar and Prester John had tried to cling to the shore and had been washed back into the bay. Baltizar nearly drowned but John had caught him and kept him afloat as the next wave carried them out again, and north towards the river. John had swum for it, towing the captain by the hair, more frightened of drowning than of crocodiles. An attempt to climb the high banks near the shore had been made futile by the current and waves, and Prester John finally found a branch he could climb on, holding the half-drowned Baltizar by the collar. When the captain had recovered his wits and stamina he too had clung there, and so they spent the night.

I was sure that Oliver had drowned before me, and Jack was convinced that it was Chips in the jaws of a hungry bull that he had watched pass from behind a tree on the morning after the blow. They had lit the fire every night in the hope of drawing survivors, but it seemed we were the last of the crew.

The ridgeline, as I had suspected, was free of the bigger predators. The men had survived on water and some fruits that grew near the edge. We were nearly unarmed. Baltizar and I had our knives, Jack a stave of sorts, and Prester John a cutlass. Baltizar also possessed a pistol and some powder and a few balls that he'd had in a pouch when the storm struck. They had dried the powder as best they could in the sun, and Baltizar had loaded the weapon with no idea whether the powder would fire.

We decided to wait a day or so for me to regain my strength, and then follow the ridge towards shore to see if we could find any other supplies that had been washed into the forest.

It was dawn of the third day when we climbed down the rubble to the forest a half-mile from shore. Baltizar and I cut staves for ourselves, and Prester John drew his cutlass. As we walked, I noticed that Baltizar's limp had become much more pronounced, and that he needed to rest as often as I did.

On shore we formed a line across, sweeping at first the beach, then the forest's edge, and then a strip of forest itself. We found a few yards of canvas and the cordage I had spotted on the morning after the storm. I also recovered my journal, intact and fairly dry. We found two empty casks, Baltizar's hat, a bent cutlass and, on the final sweep, the longboat.

It was overturned on a small bush in the forest, intact except for a torn strip of gunwale and missing oarlock. We righted it and stood about it, silent before our salvation. A dozen men might need a thirty-foot craft to carry them, but four men could sail in a twenty-foot longboat, and carry enough water to boot.

We became slightly mad in our excitement, trying to drag it immediately towards shore. At our first stop for breath, after fifty feet or so of wild stumbling, Baltizar found his wits. His limp had grown worse, so he stood watch while the three of us fixed ropes and dragged the boat with a steady pull towards shore. The sun was lowering into the forest behind us when we set the bow end in the bay. Had we not been driven to sail that night, I suspect that we might have all made it to sea—possibly all slept aboard while anchored in some way out in the bay, and then made our last preparations in the morning. But there was not one of us that wished to spend another night on that cursed island.

So, in our hurry, in our fear, in our weakness and exhaustion, we split up. The captain and Prester John took to the forest's edge to cut a sapling for a mast and for oars, and Jack and I filled our casks with water and gathered some fruit.

Baltizar and John had the mast aboard, and had returned to the forest when Jack and I dumped the last load of fruit into the boat. The sun dropped behind the jungle entirely, leaving us in a grey dusk, and it was then that the hungry bull stepped out of the jungle.

I had been expecting hunters all day but had given little thought to the larger beasts. They had always skirted us when we were in a group, but now we were split into twos, a more tempting number. The beast sniffed the air and made directly towards Baltizar and Prester John, who had just stepped out of the forest, each with a sapling on their shoulder.

In the next moments I would see the bravest sight in my life, and the most cowardly. The reptile lowered its great head and charged, reaching the buccaneers in scant seconds. The pirates *stood their ground*. Baltizar dropped his sapling and drew his pistol and Prester John's cutlass, which he'd still had in his belt, and fired the pistol directly into the face of the creature. The fouled powder flared hugely in the dusk, and the hungry bull stumbled in its charge, directly into the huge sapling that Prester John swung with preternatural strength, catching the monster alongside the skull and staggering it so that it almost fell.

Almost. The beast regained its balance and reared back to strike and Baltizar was alongside it, driving his cutlass to the hilt beneath the reptile's small arms. Prester John brought his club around again, this time across a leg, and, miraculously, the creature toppled to the sand.

It took longer to tell than the happening.

It lived, it tried to rise, and the two buccaneers backed away warily, Baltizar staggering. I knew their thoughts: that the cutlass wound must be mortal, and could they get safely enough away from its death throes, a haunch of that beast would give us meat for our voyage when it finally died.

And then the nightmare burst from the forest.

I knew there were a dozen large beasts we had not seen yet in our habitation of the island, for we'd seen many types of tracks. But we had found no evidence of what came out of the jungle, something from beyond the ridgeline, something from beyond the darkness of human imagination lunging towards us. It was leviathan, behemoth, dragon.

The creature was related to the hungry bull in the way a mastiff is cousin to the terrier. Its great head was as long as a man, its teeth marlinspikes, its forelegs muscled and clawed, its longer hind legs propelling it yards at a stride, massive, and so huge it picked up the hungry bull by the neck and crushed the life from it in a moment. And then the behemoth dropped it and turned to the two men on the beach.

I was leaning on the boat, stunned by the sudden action on the shore, and had been ready to shout with triumph when Baltizar and Prester John had downed the great reptile. Now I was frozen in terror, aware only of Jack trying to pull the boat into the bay, shouting for me to help, but I could not look away.

Baltizar and John turned and ran towards us, wise enough to know that they could not face this *thing*, that nothing short of a ship's full broadside of cannon could slow it, and in three steps Baltizar stumbled and fell to his knees.

John heard his cry, turned, pulled him to his feet, and that is when Baltizar stabbed his dagger into Prester John's belly. Jack cried out something crude and outraged. And as Prester John sank to the sand, Baltizar staggered and stumbled towards us. The great beast's jaws closed on Prester John and it stopped to toss the poor fellow back into its gullet, as a bulldog would swallow a sausage.

I spun towards Jack, our eyes met in a simple understanding, and we pushed the longboat into the bay.

We were a stone's toss into the bay when Baltizar reached the shore, screaming at us, ordering us, begging us to come back for him. Jack was paddling with a broken musket stock, myself with my hands and arms, fifty yards away when Baltizar tried to swim.

My last sight, as darkness came down upon us was a great reptile wading into the sea and plucking something from it like a gull with a crab.

18

On the end of voyaging.

We were at the mercy of the wind for twenty-three days, reduced to mixing seawater with the fresh in our casks, catching the occasional fish with handlines winnowed from our cordage and hooks made from our belt buckles. Jack was a fair sailor and not much of a navigator, but I knew enough of the stars so that he could head us northwest towards the Main when the wind allowed.

It was a merchantman out of Boston, the *Compass*, that found us at last. In three weeks I was in Boston, and in another two months back to Portsmouth. Jack had joined the crew of the merchantman, whose captain had not questioned our story of being shipwrecked privateers, especially bolstered by my tales of serving on the *Worcester*.

We told no one of the island, and most especially did not speak of its inhabitants.

I have written this account because such an account needs to be written. I have had qualms about keeping this, and my journal, private, for worry that someone might chance upon the island again, unprepared. But with its dangerous approach, reef- and rock-guarded bay, it is unlikely that others might land there. In two centuries of navigation ours is the only ship that I have found that landed there.

I find it much more worrisome that someone might *seek the place out*, and so my silence.

Afterword

Dr. Christopher Lemuel, a respected physician and naturalist, and a member of the Royal Society, died in 1705. He never again left England, but published several books on British fauna, including a work on British reptiles where he discusses connections between environment and size among species a century and a half before Darwin and Huxley.

There is obviously something more than a little self-serving in his unwillingness to publish his story of an island populated by dinosaurs, a word that would not be coined until the century after his death. It was likely that he would not have been believed and, of course, if it had become general knowledge that he had been a passenger and served as a doctor among pirates, he might have found himself in prison or with a noose around his neck.

Of the island, we would expect that in the age of modern sea voyages and with the use of satellite imagery it would have been located, but alas, this has not happened. The most likely theory is that the island no longer exists, the second that it exists but that the dinosaurs do not. As to the first, Lemuel describes an island that is mostly marshy lowlands— that it sank into the sea slowly, or because of an earthquake such as the one that rocked Jamaica in 1692, is fairly likely. That the island might have had a unique microclimate that was healthy for the dinosaurs, but changed as weather patterns shifted over the last few centuries, is also not an impossibility.

Strangely enough, what is less likely is that Dr. Lemuel is lying. He describes so carefully and accurately (and in more detail in his journal) the appearance and habits of several species of Cretaceous dinosaurs of South America, that there is little doubt that he found living, breathing beasts that were supposed to have gone extinct over sixty million years ago. And he described these animals centuries before scientists would find their *fossils*.

CPSIA information can be obtained
at www.ICGtesting.com
Printed in the USA
BVHW030642120121
597539BV00023B/132